I0692496

James Gibbons

Miscellaneous and patriotic poems

James Gibbons

Miscellaneous and patriotic poems

ISBN/EAN: 9783337306403

Printed in Europe, USA, Canada, Australia, Japan

Cover: Foto ©Andreas Hilbeck / pixelio.de

More available books at **www.hansebooks.com**

MISCELLANEOUS

AND

...RIOTIC POEMS.

By Ja... ...ons.

Oh! harp of my cou...
  In vain would the...
Thou'rt the gift of o...
  Thy music still ...

PRINTED FOR PRIVATE CIRCULATION.
1870.

INDEX.

6   Index.

TO MRS. MARY HUNEKER.

MY DEAR DAUGHTER:

In accordance with a long-expressed wish of the family, that I should gather my fugitive pieces, and put them in a more durable form, I do so now reluctantly, my principal fear being criticism. That objection, however, is of no account, as the book is not for sale, being intended only for a few friends, as a memento, and therefore beyond the reach of public judgment. As you are well aware, these pages were written amidst the busy and weary hours of labor, without preparation or regard to the future; they should, therefore, be lightly dealt with on that account.

To you, my dear daughter Mary, I dedicate these pages, as a lasting pledge of love and regard of your affectionate father, JAMES GIBBONS.

POEMS AND SONGS.

'TIS SAD TO SAY FAREWELL.

'Tis sad to say farewell, love :
  Thy absence gives me pain ;
'Tis sad to say farewell to those
  We long to meet again.
'Twas thus I mused in sadness
  And fondly gazed on thee,
When the stars hung out their silver lamps
  Above the dark blue sea.

Peace seemed to breathe around us,
  With music from each wave ;
The moon looked with her silver smile
  Down on the light she gave.
This was the sweetest vision
  Ere came across my view ;
'Twas neither moon nor ocean—
  The charm was lent by you.

I would recall those pleasures,
  And stand again by thee,
Where light and shadow would reflect
  Their own sweet smile on me.
Those happy hours have faded
  Like glories of the past,
Or dreams that fill us with delight
  Too beautiful to last.

SWEET LILLY BELL.

THE dew is on the rose, love;
　　The blossom's on the tree;
The little birds are singing, love,
　　Their sweetest notes for thee.
I swear by bird and blossom, love,
　　By mountain, brook, and dell,
My heart is ever thine, love,
　　My own sweet Lilly Bell.

Sweet Lilly, lovely Lilly Bell,
　　Where e'er my footsteps roam,
My thoughts return to thee, love,
　　Like weary wand'rer home,
To gaze on thy sweet face, love,
　　Whose smile I love so well,
And worship at thy shrine, love,
　　My own sweet Lilly Bell.

Thou star of all my hopes, love,
　　May thy lustre ne'er decline;
May peace in gentle murmurs breathe
　　On that sweet face of thine.
May fortune strew with fairest flow'rs,
　　From mountain-nook or dell,
Around the path of my fond love,
　　My own sweet Lilly Bell.

————

A DREAM OF BEAUTY.

I HAD a dream of beauty, love—
　　A nymph rose from the sea,
And standing by my side, she cast
　　Her sweetest smile on me;

She had no wreath upon her head,
　Nor gems wrought in her hair,
But stood in all her loveliness,
　A Queen of beauty there.

Her every look and every smile
　Had beauty in each tone,
And when she spoke, her flute-like voice
　Was music all her own ;
She sweetly said, " Why are you sad ?
　Why fling your harp away ?
Its tones will murmur back to thee
　The love of life's young day."

And oh that look ! and oh that voice !
　They played the wizard's part.
And standing in the pale moonlight
　She soothed my stricken heart.
When I awoke, it was no dream ;
　I stood beside the sea ;
And thy sweet smile had taught my heart
　To sing of naught but thee.

I AM VERY SAD TO-NIGHT.

I MET thee in the sweetest month
　That blooms in all the year,
When loneliness sat on my heart
　Both desolate and drear ;
Thy smile was bright and beautiful,
　And filled me with delight.
But oh ! I cannot sing those lays :
　I am very sad to-night.

I will not sing—I cannot sing,
  Those loving lays to thee;
For, oh! thou art a cruel bird
  To fly away from me;
Pulse of my heart! it cannot be
  That thou wouldst cast a blight
On this fond heart that sings to thee:
  I am very sad to-night.

I'll sing for thee my sweetest lays,
  Lays I have never sung;
In loving thee I quite forgot   .
  I was no longer young.
Why was it willed that I should meet
  A face so pure and bright?
My fair-haired love, I must confess
  I am very sad to-night.

THE VOICE OF HER I LOVE.

Tell me whither can I go,
  Ah! whither can I rove,
· Where no reflection brings to mind
  The voice of her I love?
They tell me Summer's beautiful
  With flowers fresh and gay;
That little birds are singing sweet—
  I heed not what they say.
The trees may blossom into bloom,
  With songsters in the grove;
No music e'er can charm me
  Save the voice of her I love.

I LOVE THEE BETTER NOW.

COME list, my own dear Mary,
　While I sing life's cares away,
And warble o'er love's early notes,
　Bright dreams of life's young day,
When, heart to heart, we plighted, love,
　Affection's tender vow :
I loved thee then, my Mary dear ;
　I love thee better now.

We'll wander forth at evening,
　On the banks of yonder stream,
Whose waters gush in melody
　Beneath the bright moonbeam ;
And there I'll sing, my Mary,
　Of my first, my early vow :
I loved thee then, my Mary dear ;
　I love thee better now.

I'll sing to thee, my Mary,
　Of pleasures that are past,
Of scenes, my own dear Mary,
　Too beautiful to last,
When youth and beauty were thine own,
　Nor shadow on thy brow :
I loved thee then, my Mary dear ;
　I love thee better now.

THE NEGLECTED GRAVE.

BEHOLD the lone grave of her I respected !
　Who quietly sleeps in her cold house of clay ;
While living abused : ah ! in death how neglected --
　No friend comes the tribute of sorrow to pay.

No stone marks the spot where her ashes repose,
 Yet Nature in kindness is sharing her bloom;
The daisy and primrose their beauty disclose,
 And perfume the breezes that sigh o'er her tomb.

Yes! Nature, still true to the laws of creation,
 Remembering the wants of the lowliest slave,
In the absence of wealth and all vain ostentation,
 Strews with fresh flowers the loneliest grave.

Sleep on, beloved friend! thee I'd not awaken,
 As now thou art sleeping the sleep of the free;
Thou art but forgot—then thou'dst be forsaken,
 And cast like a wreck upon life's troubled sea.

THE DARK BLUE SEA.

I stood on the shore of the dark blue sea,
 And gazed o'er the mighty deep,
As wave on wave dashed wildly free,
 Where storms their vigils keep.

Each wave leapt wild, fitfully wild,
 With a loud unearthly roar,
As billow on billow, like mountains piled,
 Were broke on the pearly shore.

I viewed the sea fowl dart away,
 Then wheel round its watery home,
And dip its wing in the silver spray
 That rose from the boiling foam.

Tell me, ah! tell me, thou dark blue sea,
 Why Death sits on each wave,
And strikes with his dart the brave and free,
 With the ocean for their grave?

What magical power, say, mighty deep,
   Heaves thy waves on high,
And soothes thee to rest, like a babe to sleep,
   When the wind has ceased to sigh?

The power that I have, said the dark blue sea,
   I wield without control;
I move by the power of the Deity,
   As I sweep from Pole to Pole!

FAREWELL TO THE GREEN MOUNTAIN WILDWOOD.

FAREWELL to the green mountain wildwood!
   Farewell to the old trysting tree,
Whose shade in the morning of childhood
   Has sheltered my true love and me.
Farewell to the flower-scented pathways
   Whose memory pursues me afar;
Lost pleasures, I'll sing of your beauties
   To the sound of my dulcet guitar.

Oh! where is the brook whose soft murmur,
   Like music, rang through the lone dell,
In unison with the wood songsters
   That gave it a magical spell?
And where is my first love, my own love,
   Whose image pursues me afar,
Inspiring my strains with sad numbers
   To the sound of my dulcet guitar?

O memory! thou beautiful mirror,
   Reflecting those joys that are past,
Thy friendship is ever abiding
   Wherever our lot may be cast;

Reflecting those beautiful visions,
    The day-dreams of life's morning star,—
Lost pleasures, I'll sing of your beauties
    To the sound of my dulcet guitar.

FAREWELL, MY YOUTHFUL HOURS.

AIR—"Do you ever think of me, love."

FAREWELL, my youthful hours,
    Bright morning of life's day,
When youth, like summer flowers,
    Blooms beautiful and gay;
'Tis then each tender feeling,
    Expanding in delight,
Like angel choirs revealing
    Their music o'er the night.
Then tell me what can equal
    The morning of life's day,
When youth, like summer flowers,
    Blooms beautiful and gay?

Oh! I sigh for those fond hours
    When my love sat by my knee,
'Neath the shade of spreading bowers,
    And softly sang to me;
While zephyrs sweet were swelling
    Their music through the grove,
And feathered songsters telling
    Their tales of artless love.
Then tell me what can equal
    The morning of life's day,
When youth, like summer flowers,
    Blooms beautiful and gay?

THE ORPHAN BOY'S LAMENT.

AIR—"The harp that once through Tara's halls."

To the shores of Erin's lovely isle my parents bid adieu;
  Bright were their hopes and glad their hearts with free-
      dom's shores in view;
Religion was their guiding star—the Christian's hope
      their joy,—
Ah! woe is me! they sleep in death; I'm a homeless
      orphan boy.

Sad was the night and drear the hour my father breathed
      his last;
With grief my mother pined away—her sorrows now are
      past;
And I am lone and desolate, without one ray of joy—
A stranger in a stranger's land—a homeless orphan boy.

Light of my eyes! pulse of my heart! my mother, where
      art thou?
In vain I scan each female face to find thy placid brow;
In vain I seek a mother's smile—oh grief without alloy!
Each stranger's look reminds me I'm a lonely orphan boy.

The night winds sigh above those hearts that loved me
      true and well;
Those eyes are dim and motionless, closed in that dreary
      cell;
That voice is hushed, forever hushed, that welcomed me
      with joy;—   [boy.
It ne'er can cheer the hopeless heart of the lonely orphan

They tell me that my parents live in mansions pure and
      bright,
Where angels chant eternal hymns amidst celestial light;
That we will meet, no more to part from never ending joy:
Then I'll forget the sad lament of the lonely orphan boy.

ADDRESS OF THE LITTLE BIRDS OF FRANKLIN SQUARE TO THE LITTLE BIRDS OF WASHINGTON SQUARE.

To our friends of the Washington Square we send greeting,
And highly approve of your concerts and meeting.
In person your concerts we cannot attend,
But hope you'll accept the kind wishes we send;—
Highly engaged, while the weather is fair,
To sing to our friends of Franklin Square.
The winter is gone with its chills and its colds,
And Nature her beauties, her riches unfolds;—
Beautiful May, in her gayest attire,
Sweet scenes of enchantment our songs shall inspire;
Gratitude's feelings shall burden our song,
And sweeten the notes that we'll pour to the throng
Who visit our Square and sit 'neath our bowers,
Reviving their spirits from fountain and flowers.
When the sun is declining far, far in the west,
And zephyrs are fanning all nature to rest,
We'll pour forth our song in sweet accents of love
To the Author of All in His mansions above.
At morning we'll pour forth our song on the breeze,
After sipping the dew-drops from flowers and trees,
When Aurora refulgent is gilding the skies,
And morning to gladness is opening her eyes;
Oh! then will we warble our song with delight,
And bid a good-bye to the sorrowing night—
We'll skip round the fountain and merrily sing,
And wash 'neath its shower the dust from our wing!
We invite all our friends of every condition
To visit our concerts—no charge for admission;
Equality's rules we shall ever obey,
The strictest attention to ladies we pay,
And hope they'll attend us, all blooming and fair,

And grace by their presence the Franklin Square.
Our fountain is throwing its waters as free
As the wind o'er the forest, or the waves of the sea;
And our Square is attired in the richest of green,
With the butterfly skipping about like a queen,
Inviting her friends to a supper of dew,
With the locust and grasshopper, going two and two;
The firefly's here, and he carries a light
To show to his friends that he visits at night.
So Nature, uniting a harmonious strain,
Is pouring her music o'er mountain and plain !
Dear friends, we will bid you a happy adieu,
And soon hope to have an epistle from you.

THE LITTLE BIRDS' FAREWELL TO
FRANKLIN SQUARE.

FAREWELL, ah ! farewell to thee, bright gushing fountain !
  We must bid adieu to those scenes of delight,
And hurry away to some fair, sunny mountain
  That ne'er felt the chills of a cold winter's night.

No longer the zephyrs enliven our bowers—
  The cold damp of winter is felt through the air;
Each tiny tribe, sipping dew from the flowers,
  Is vanishing away from our Franklin Square.

The butterfly's gone and the locust is dying;
  The firefly, too, has extinguished his light;
The merry grasshopper in sadness is sighing,
  Dreading the chills of a cold winter's night.

No longer we're cheered by the wild notes of gladness
  That rose on the breeze from the juvenile train.
We think of past scenes with a magical sadness,
  And nourish the hope that we'll see them again.

Why do we linger around thee, bright fountain,
    And look with regret on each green willow tree?
Ah! we think of strange scenes on some far away mountain
    That ne'er can compete with the charms of thee.

Returning again when the cold winter passes,
    We'll hail thee, bright fountain, with songs of delight,
And warble our notes to the rosy cheek'd lasses
    That sang to their loves on the cold winter's night.

TO THE STAR SPANGLED BANNER.

STILL float, spangled banner, o'er land and o'er ocean,—
    Hope of the bondsman and strength of the free;
Thy home is as free as thy own gentle motion,
    The patriot stranger is shielded by thee.

Where is the eye doth not view thee with gladness?
    Or where is the slave, be he ever so low,
Whose heart doth not bound in the midst of his sadness,
    Whose soul is not fired by liberty's glow?

Thy stars they are brilliant—an emblem of glory!
    Thy sons are protected alike under thee;
Freedom's first sires, emblazoned in story,
    Have left thee their blessing, oh flag of the free!

All nations for ages were trod by oppression—
    No day-star of freedom enlightened the world;
To freemen indignant, resisting aggression,
    Columbia's broad banner its glories unfurled.

Like Aurora's bright rays through the arches of heaven,
    Refulgent it broke o'er the sorrowing night;
The black veil of tyrants in pieces was riven,
    Displaying the eagle encircled in light.

Oh ! flag of my heart, mayst thou flourish for ever,
The terror of tyrants and hope of the slave !
May the foul fiend of discord ne'er hope to sever
The stars of our Union—oh home of the brave !

NATIONAL SONG.

Air—"Jeanette and Jenott."

Hail ! glorious land of liberty !
Thy fame has gone afar,
Cheering on the friends of freedom
'Neath thy ever beaming star ;
Thy sons, a glorious brotherhood,
Keep sentinel for thee,
As thy eagle soars in grandeur
O'er the birth-place of the free.

I love thee, fair Columbia,
For the deeds thy chiefs have done,
Who smote the foes of liberty,
And freedom's battle won ;
Then flung aloft the Stars and Stripes
Majestic and sublime,
Reflecting freedom's glorious light
To earth's remotest clime.

Hail ! glorious land of Washington !
My soul exults to see
The union Flag of Freedom
Floating peacefully o'er thee,
Dispensing joy and happiness
Around the freeman's home,
Where dire oppression finds no place
Beneath the star-lit dome.

YOU MUST NEVER, NEVER TELL.

I HAVE a little secret, love,
    A secret no one knows—
I love a fair-haired maiden,
    More beauteous than the rose;
She makes my heart more cheerful
    Than the sweetest bird that sings,
I would sit and sing beside her
    Could I borrow Cupid's wings.

Could you see that look of beauty,—
    Could you see her winning smile,—
Could you see her snow-white bosom,
    In whose heart there is no guile;
Could you see the maiden blushes,
    As the colors come and go,
You would kiss those loving roses
    For the freshness of their glow.

Now you know my little secret—
    Do not act the tell-tale part,
For you know that I must love you
    When I let you read my heart.
And this bright and beauteous image
    In my heart must ever dwell;
How I love a fair-haired beauty,
    You must never, never tell.

———

MY MUSE HAS LONG BEEN DREAMING.

My muse has long been dreaming,
    But she wakes to love and thee,
And she's sighing for you, Sallie—
    Do you ever sigh for me?

She is sighing, ever sighing,
　　Sighing to be at your side;
It were heaven but to dream it,
　　Could I say, my fair-haired bride!

Could I say it, could I sing it,
　　Could I breathe that thought to thee;
But the star of hope can never shed
　　That brilliant light on me:
Yet my thoughts still turn to thee,
　　Like a stream that sweeps along,
And my bright, my fair-haired Sallie,
　　Is the burden of my song.

TO J. S. G.

My son, I have sent you this long wished-for letter,
And deeply regret I can send you no better;
I know 'twill be welcome at all times to thee,
Being free from deception when coming from me.
This world's made up of professional wiles,
And the darkest deceit's clothed in beautiful smiles—
But why turn preacher in this sun-burning weather,
When the skin and the bone are melting together?
I envy you there, 'neath the shade of the trees,
That bow their tall branches to kiss the soft breeze,
And the flowers that spring up so gentle and sweet,
Like beautiful carpets spread under your feet;
I think that I see you trip over the lawn
To snuff the soft zephyr at day's early dawn,
Going forth in the morning among the wild bowers
When the dew-drops like pearl bespangle the flowers,
When Nature bursts forth in a song of delight
As the sun brushes forward to banish the night.

How glorious the scene at the day's early dawn
When night has departed in mist from the lawn,
And calmness and quiet are reigning around,
While Nature seems hushed in devotions profound,
Paying homage to God in the stillness of morn,
Rejoicing another new day has been born;
And the sun as he darts forth his light o'er the plains,
Meets Nature rejoicing in musical strains;
And the tribes of the forest in magical glee
Send their voices abroad o'er valley and lea;
While the streamlet that's running so quiet and lone,
Sends its voice on the breeze with a song of its own,
And the flowers that grow by the banks of the stream,
While blushing so sweet at the sun's early beam,
Shedding their fragrance so sweetly around
That the grass-hopper dances with joy on the ground,
And the fire-fly quietly slips to the shade
And trims up her lamp for the night's masquerade!
O Summer! sweet Summer! you fill me with joy,
And the man is forgot in the thoughts of the boy,
When lightsome I sported o'er forest and glade
And plucked the wild berries that grew in the shade,
And wove me a garland of gay evergreens;
Ah! those were the fairest of life's early scenes!
But my summer is past like a false lover's vow,
And the shadows of life cast a shade o'er my brow.
Rejoice then, my son, in this beautiful time,
For you, like the Summer, are just in your prime;
And, with Nature, rejoice in the goodness of God,
That decks with such glories the humblest sod.

NEW YEAR'S ADDRESS TO THE PATRONS OF THE NORTHERN LIBERTIES AND KENSING-TON ADVERTISER, 1852.

WE greet you, kind patrons, this happy New Year,
And wish you each blessing you value most dear.
As the Old Year has passed like a shadow away,
Or a beautiful cloud on a bright summer day,
Or the sun as he peacefully sinks in the west,
Bidding good-night to a world he has blest;
So the Old Year has vanished away from our view,
And leaves in its place the New Year, Fifty-Two.
Dear reader, we think that, in stringing some rhymes,
It would not be amiss should we speak of the times:
From the past and the present there's much we may learn,
And in passing events we can easily discern
The blessing of peace that encircles our shores,
Where the eagle of freedom triumphantly soars,
And our broad banner floating in glory unfurled,
Giving hope, aye, and light, to a down-trodden world!
See Europe convulsed like an upheaving sea,
And humanity crushed in attempts to be free;
While despots, like demons, together unite
To bury the day-star of liberty's light,
Declaring the people know not their own good,
And to save them from ruin, baptize them in blood.
Oh! for the day when the millions shall rise,
And the shouts of their vict'ries ascend to the skies;
When Truth, like a giant, shall sweep from her path
The foes of mankind in the day of her wrath,
And restore to the nations each long cherished right
That for ages lay buried in slavery's night.

Our country next claims all we have to say,
And prompt at her shrine our homage we pay.

All hail, Columbia! land of liberty!
The exile's home from ruthless tyranny;
Thy "Stars and Stripes" float out on every breeze,
Beloved on land, respected on the seas;
Astonished nations hail thee with delight,
As thy bright banner bursts upon their sight!
Thy hardy sons still cultivate the soil;
A bounteous God rewards industrious toil;
Thy fertile fields luxuriant crops bestow;
Thy thousand streams in peaceful murmurs flow;
Thy mountains stored with ore of every kind;
Thy countless schools to cultivate the mind;
No bloated lord, no upstart potentate,
Assails our freedom or enslaves the State;
But peace and plenty, handmaids of the free,
Hath bounteous Heaven freely given to thee.
Freemen! value what your freedom cost,
And prize the boon ere that fair prize be lost;
Cast faction from you as your sires have done,
Who changed a tyrant for a Washington;
Sustain those laws kind Heaven did bestow
To make our land a paradise below.
Should Freedom's temple totter on its base,
And anarchy unmask its hideous face,
Then blame those tools by party faction made,
Who laugh at justice, and our laws degrade.
For us, we cling to Union's glorious car,
With truth and justice for our guiding star,
And take our stand for right, no matter where,
To guard each trust committed to our care.

May heavenly blessings fall like summer showers
Around you, patrons, till life's latest hours,
And guide you safely o'er life's dreary road,
In peace with man and friendship with your God;

And when the hour-glass of your time has run,
And all your labors, like your life, are done,
May guardian angels light your onward way
To the blest home of God's eternal day.

A VOICE FROM THE NORTH.—1853.

DEDICATED TO EX-PRESIDENT TYLER.

My Southern brother!—oh! list to my story:
'Tis the fame of our country, her triumphs and glory,
When freemen stood up against foreign oppression,
And bravely and boldly resisted aggression;
Midst hope and despair, in our country's dark hour,
They measured their strength with the tyrant's dread power
Who came in his pride o'er Atlantic's wild water,
Proclaiming his laws amid carnage and slaughter.
My brother! the thought of the past rushes o'er me,
And the image of Washington looms up before me,
As he stood by our fathers with the love of a mother
And looked in their face with the look of a brother;
When, column on column, he led them to battle
Midst clashing of sabres and cannons' loud rattle,
And humbled the pride of the loud vaunting foeman
With the courage and prowess of Liberty's yeoman.
O bright be their names in the pages of story
Who flung round our country a halo of glory,
While yielding their lives up to Liberty's labor!
They carved out their fame with the bright hilted sabre,
And onward, still onward, together united,
To God and their country their vows were all plighted,
And raised up an altar, lit Liberty's fire;
God strengthened their arms, their souls did inspire,
And blest them one people, that nothing should sever
While their forests were green or their lands held a river,

That the nations afar from their altar should borrow
A ray to enlighten their pathway of sorrow.
Ah! those were the days when no flippant debater
Dare stand forth unmasked in the garb of a traitor;
When truth shook the land in a voice loud as thunder,
And severed the chain of oppression asunder.
My brother, the truth of the great Revolution,
That gave us a Union and free Constitution,
Shall triumph o'er treason and treason's dark doing,
O'er higher law factions, who rule but to ruin
Our country and fame we so fervently cherish,
Hopes and a home for which freemen would perish;
The fate of an Arnold, in infamy sleeping
Where crime and corruption their vigils are keeping,
Shall brand as her own the fell spirit of treason
That wars against country, religion, and reason.
My brother, rejoice! see the bright path before us!
The fair sun of Freedom in beauty beams o'er us,
And the Star Spangled Banner in glory unfurled
Inspiring the hopes of a down-trodden world;
And our eagle soars up through the blue vaults of heaven;
While God in his mercy all blessings has given,
And peace, like a dove, spreads her wings of protection
O'er the great and the small with a mother's affection.
Then green be your fields and your fair sunny valleys,
And strong be your son who for liberty rallies;
Thrice blest be their vows that for freedom were plighted
Around the fair flag of a people united,
For ours is the freest, the happiest nation
E'er smiled 'neath the sun since the dawn of creation.

A DREAM.

Messrs. Editors:—As many of your readers believe,

like myself, that the age of dreams is not past, the following may not be uninteresting to them :—

Travelling through the lovely valley of the Mississippi, and being fatigued, I laid me down to rest; lulled by the gentle hum of insects, and soothed by the delicious air of a Southern clime, I soon fell asleep. Oh God! the vision that presented itself to my horrified sight harrows my very soul, even as I now write. Thousands and tens of thousands of the ghastly corpses of the Union and Confederate armies appeared, hurrying to and fro, forming in brigades and battalions, far as the eye could reach, a countless host. They advance in line of battle—to fight? No—they embrace; in death their eyes have opened, and they now see that they have been the victims of cursed ambition. Presently two majestic forms appear, advancing to the head of the column : one, the Goddess of Liberty, robed in black, holding in one hand a scroll, on her arm a broken shield; the other you cannot mistake—it is the "Father of his Country," sorrow and anguish stamped on his noble brow. After sorrowfully surveying her slaughtered children, the Goddess of Liberty cried out, or rather wailed the following :

We are coming, Abraham Lincoln,
  From mountain, wood, and glen ;
We are coming, Abraham Lincoln,
  With the ghosts of murdered men.
Yes! we're coming, Abraham Lincoln,
  With curses loud and deep,
That will haunt you in your waking
  And disturb you in your sleep.

There's blood upon your garments,
  There's guilt upon your soul,
For the lust of ruthless soldiers
  You let loose without control ;

Your dark and wicked doings
  A God of Mercy sees,
And the wail of homeless children
  Is heard on every breeze.

There's sadness in our dwellings,
  And the cry of wild despair
From broken hearts and ruined homes
  Breaks on the midnight air;
While sorrow spreads her funeral pall
  O'er this once happy land;
For brother meets, in deadly strife,
  A brother's battle brand.

With desolation all around,
  Our dead lie on the plains;
You're coming, Abraham Lincoln,
  With manacles and chains,
To subjugate the white man
  And set the negro free—
By the blood of all these murdered men,
  This curse can never be!

You may call your black battalions
  To aid your sinking cause,
And substitute your vulgar jokes
  For liberty and laws.
No! by the memory of our fathers,
  By those green, unnumbered graves,
We'll perish on ten thousand fields
  Ere *we* become your slaves!

Hark! hear you not the battle crash—
  Seest not the lightning's gleam?
The earth drinks up a brother's blood—
  O God! it is no dream!

                    Phila. Evening Journal, April 22, 1863

THE RUMSELLER.

UNHAPPY man! child of ignoble fame!
Lost to honor, honesty, and shame;
To every feeling, every virtue dead—
Destroying souls, for whom a Saviour bled.
What wide-spread ruin and domestic strife,
The hapless orphan, with the injured wife;
Your wicked traffic thousands yearly kills
With deadly potions from the cursed stills!
Can you escape that last and fatal curse,
Reserved for those who keep the guilty purse,
When vice and virtue take a last farewell—
For virtue, heaven; the other doomed to hell?
What hand can paint, with colors bright and true,
The crafty cunning of that selfish crew—
Their low deceit and avaricious wiles,
With outstretched hand and hypocritic smiles;
Their splendid bar-rooms, furniture profuse,
With stands erect to hold the daily news.
Here chairs and tables stand in ample rows,
For lazy loafers, dice, and dominoes;
There gilded pictures from the walls are strung,
To suit the fancy of the old and young;
There naked statues, raised a little high,
To gratify the vain and vulgar eye!
Yonder a table stands in bold relief,
And well supplied with musty cheese and beef;
A box of sand is kept in constant use,
Retaining showers of tobacco juice;
Vile liquor flowing like a fountain spring,
While horrid oaths from every quarter ring;
There, all around, is one unmeaning hum,
The wild effusions of debasing rum.

The landlord's happy while the goblets flow—
His source of wealth, the cause of other's woe!
He laughs and jokes at all he hears and sees,
And soon grows fat in indolence and ease.
His wife, content before a smiling grate;
His foppish sons like ministers of state;
His daughters, too, in trappings sweep along,
And nightly mingle in the giddy throng
At splendid ball-rooms, and such giddy shows,
With every pleasure ill-got wealth bestows.

Reverse the picture—view the other side—
Behold the prop, the basis of his pride!
See yon poor dolt, asleep behind the door,
Bereft of shame, quite senseless on the floor—
Deludèd wretch! half mad with alcohol,
Forgets his wife, the partner of his soul,
Who now sits weeping by the midnight lamp,
Her sickly chamber dismal, cold, and damp;
A broken heart—a sad, dejected face—
Her hopes all blasted in that hellish place
Where every tie, both human and divine,
Is now forgot amidst triumphant crime.
The famished children to their mother cry,
Who to her babe is humming lullaby,
While tears are flowing from her burning eyes—
Her bosom bursting with continued sighs;
She soothes her babe with sorrow's plaintive hum,
Her last fond hope, that all's not spent for rum!
And, weary nature panting for repose,
She sinks in sleep, to dream of coming woes.

Remorseless man! those burning tears that flow
Have stamped on you the brand of human woe!

A WELCOME TO FATHER MATHEW.

We welcome thee, Father, and hail thee with gladness!
   Thy coming is joy to the abject and low;
And the grief-stricken mother, long sighing in sadness,
   Beholds in thee, Father, a balm for her woe.
The wife who sat pining in sad destitution,
   Has sighed for thy coming—she sighed not in vain;
For thy voice has called forth, from his haunts of pollution,
   The hope of her heart to her bosom again.

Thrice welcome, lov'd Father, for thine is the glory
   To labor where sorrow her victim controls;
And men, as they read of thy mission in story,
   Will say of a truth thou'rt the shepherd of souls.
The poor and the wretched that withered in sorrow,
   And sighed in their hearts from life's ills to be free;
Who ne'er had a hope of a brighter to-morrow,
   Have found, beloved Father, a solace in thee.

We welcome thee, Father, with freemen's devotion!
   And bid thee God-speed in our Temperance cause;
We'll aid and sustain thee with heartfelt emotion;
   For virtue's the guardian of freedom and laws.
Our Stars and our Stripes are in glory surrounded,
   Floating freely and fairly o'er Liberty's dome;
Reposing beneath them, with feelings unbounded,
   We bid thee thrice welcome to Liberty's home!

THE OULD HOUSE THAT STOOD AT THE CORNER OF FRONT AND NOBLE STREETS.

It's meself, shure, that had a most illegant dhrame
About an ould woman, a witch ov a dame,
I saw wringing her hands, as she cried—"What a shame!
   Arrah, where's the ould house at the corner?"

"Bedad, my ould lady, the house is pulled down,
And the raisin that's given is certainly sound :
They say that the public wanted the ground
    Of the 'Ould House' that stood at the corner ;

"So the house is pulled down and the flure gone to sticks,
And the walls so long standin' are morthar and bricks—
Be japers, ould woman, it's a horrible fix
    They have made ov the house at the corner !"

"And the oyster man's gone! arrah, where did he go?"—
"Be the powers ov Moll Kelly, meself doesn't know ;
But I'm towld he would make a most illegant show
    For Barnum to put in a corner."

"And the oysters are gone—och their loss I deplore !
They were always brought fresh from the eastern shore ;
Fried, roasted, or stewed, we'll see them no more
    Handled so *clean* at the corner !"

THE GRAND DISPLAY OF FIREWORKS AT BROAD AND MARKET STREETS.

Fourth of July, 1851.

DEAR reader!—ah ! you missed the sight
    Of that great celebration,
When our City Fathers gave a fete
    By cards of invitation,
To every mother's son around
    Who loved his country's glory
To come to Broad and Market Streets,
    A famous place in story ;

That mighty doings would be there
  With fireworks and with rockets,
And many other things beside,
  Paid from the people's pockets.
With anxious look of hope and fear,
  And glorious expectation,
The good folks hurried off in crowds
  To see the celebration.

A living mass thronged all the streets
  Of gentlemen and ladies,
And mothers running out of breath
  To please their little babies;
Old men grew young, and hopped along,
  Forgetful of their labors,
Trod on the toes and tore the clothes
  Of many friends and neighbors.

I thought I was a shingle, sir,
  I got so great a squeezing,
And some were six times worse than I
  With coughing and with sneezing,
While Paddy Whack ran up and down,
  And cried out, "blood and thunder!
Sure, Barnum ought to cage this crowd
  And show it as a wonder."

Some pushed and crushed, and some fell down,
  And some could stand no longer,
While some drank ginger-pop and rum
  To make their spirits stronger.
The clock struck ten, and yet no works
  Of fire showed their faces;
And many wished for stools and chairs
  · To have more easy places.

The best of patience must wear out,
   When angry passion gathers ;
And many an impious prayer was heaped
   Upon our City Fathers ;
While bitter moan and sullen groan
   Were heard in different quarters,
From men who bravely stood their ground,
   Like Fox's famous martyrs.

At last the City Fathers came,
   Each mounted on a charger ;
And, Billy dear, it's truth I tell—
   They made the crowd much larger ;
The Mayor he wore a three cocked hat,
   And led the Corporation—
You'd swear it was John Gilpin's ghost
   That *came* by invitation.

My very heart was like to break
   To see his Honor rising
To make a very little speech,
   By way of sermonizing ;
When some unruly dog cried out,
   "Oh, speak a little louder !"
"Ah me !" his Honor meekly said,
   "*The rain has wet the powder.*"

I WILL REMEMBER THEE, LOVE.

I WILL remember thee, love !
   I never can forget
The moon-lit sea, the surf-bound shore,
   The happy time we met.

I never can forget, love;
  I think I see thee now
As youth and beauty sweetly smiled
  Upon thy placid brow.

I'll think of thee at dawn, love,
  When Nature's face is fair,
And breathe for thee at vesper time
  A blessing and a prayer.
I'll weave a wreath for thee, love,
  Of poetry and song,
And deck thee with the fairest flowers
  That to my muse belong.

THE GREEN OLD HILLS OF IRELAND.

Ye green old hills of Ireland!
  How beautiful ye stand
Like pyramids of emerald
  In some mysterious land,
Wherein celestial spirits
  May make their blest abode;
Ye green old hills of Ireland—
  Ye glorious work of God!

The rainbow has its beauties,
  Yet they fade before the sun;
And the fairest flower droops and dies
  Ere half the year is done;
But the green old hills of Ireland
  Mock the iron hand of time;—
Their emerald summits tower aloft
  Majestic and sublime.

Why stand ye, hills of Ireland,
  Thus robed in bright array,
While millions pine, in want and woe,
  Their weary lives away?
Ay! withering 'neath oppression's yoke,
  To fill ignoble graves—
Ten thousand deaths were better far
  Than wear the badge of slaves!

See! Freedom, resting on her shield,
  With terror stands aghast!
Disgusted with a war of words,
  She's gazing on the past:
"Go! hereditary bondsmen, go!
  And gaze on Clontarf's plains;
But tread not on its sacred soil,
  While wearing Saxon chains."

Thus mused a son of Erin,
  While pensively he thought
On many a blood-stained battle-field
  His countrymen had fought.
Oh! the glorious days of Brian
  Fling back their hallowed shades
Round the green old hills of Ireland,
  Whose shamrock never fades.

Oh! would the grave give back those chiefs
  Ye had in days of yore,
Whose prowess drove the Northmen
  From your consecrated shore!
Oh! then the cry of freedom rang
  Through mountain pass and glen;
And echoed round your cloud-capt hills
  The shouts of warrior men.

TO THE REPEALERS OF IRELAND.

Has your noble vessel stranded?
  Then awake your gallant crew,
And show admiring nations
  What a daring host can do;
Throw overboard those sentinels
  That slumbered on their post,
And jeopardised your country's rights
  Upon the Saxon coast.

Arise! put up your helm,
  And trim your bark for sea—
There are hurricanes and quicksands
  In the pathway of the free;
Nor pause nor falter on your way
  To gaze on dangers past;
Run up your ancient green flag,
  Aye, and nail it to the mast!

Arise! and gird ye for the fray,
  With helmet, spear, and shield;
Your nationhood can ne'er be won,
  Save on the battle-field!
The glories of Tyrconnell
  Beamed forth supremely grand,
When Ulster's frowning battlements
  Displayed the Red Right Hand.

Why stand like paltry suppliants?
  'Tis abject, meanly vile,
Unworthy of your fathers
  Or the genius of your isle;
Your wars of words are powerless—
  They want the flashing eye,
That should reflect the brave resolve
  To nobly do or die.

While faith and hope are in your souls,
　　Be true to virtue's cause :
Your motto—"God and Liberty,"
　　Your country and her laws.
There's ambush in each mountain pass
　　And calmness in the glen,
And courage still unconquered
　　In the breasts of Irish men.

———

TO THE GREEN FLAG OF THE 3RD REGIMENT OF THE VOLUNTEERS OF '82.

Presented to William S. O'Brien by the citizens of Dublin, April 15th, 1848.

ALL hail, thrice glorious banner !
　　Pride of our Volunteers !
You fill my soul with bounding hopes
　　And thoughts of better years ;
You fling the shadows of the past
　　In glory round the hand
That holds you, with a chieftain's grasp,
　　To meet the battle brand.

All hail, Kinkora's brilliant star !
　　Son of a kingly race !
You'll guard that flag in battle strife,
　　And shield it from disgrace ;
Its honor shall be safely kept,—
　　You've pledged a brave man's word
To light the path to Liberty
　　With Brian's trusty sword !

Up! Ireland, at your tyrants!
  Is the cry of thinking men;—
Each green hill-side's a fortress,
  There's a stronghold in each glen;
The mountain-pass and wild morass
  Are Nature's barricades;—
Up! Ireland, at your tyrants!
  Charge like Fontenoy's brigades!

Oh! how I love the battle crash,
  When sturdy yeomen strike!
Oh! how I love the music
  From the ringing of the pike!
The freeman's hope is shining steel
  When tyranny invades;
The path to Ireland's liberty
  Is with her bold brigades.

Oh! how I love the thundering cheer
  That echoes to the sky,
And sweeps along victorious lines,
  As broken columns fly!
Oh, Erin! gird thee for the fray—
  Bring forth your brave platoons,
And crush the Saxon myrmidons
  Beneath your bold dragoons!

ERIN GRAMACHREE.

Air—"With a helmet on his brow."

Oh! give to me the western breeze
  That sweeps along the deep,
And heaves on high the briny seas
  Where mermaids never sleep;

And waft me to Hibernia's shore,
    Where hearts are brave and free,—
I'll never, never leave thee more,
    Old Erin Gramachree!
                  Oh, give, &c.

I love your green and sloping hills
    By gentle breezes fann'd,
And the music of your murmuring rills,
    Your bright and pearly strand;
I love your fair and blooming maids,
    With hearts of purity,
That stray beneath thy balmy shades,
    Old Erin Gramachree!
                  Oh, give, &c.

Adieu to brave Columbia!
    My blessing be with thee—
Where the towering Eagle soars aloft—
    Bold emblem of the free!
May tyrants quail beneath the power
    Of freemen's chivalry,
Shall be the long and lasting prayer
    Of Erin Gramachree.
                  Oh, give, &c.

ERIN MAVOURNEEN, MY OWN NATIVE HOME.

AIR—" Home, sweet home."

ERIN, sweet Erin! I love your green hills,
Your pure gushing fountains and clear winding rills,
Where the lark and the linnet melodiously sing,
With the thrush and the blackbird, to welcome the Spring.
    Home, home; sweet, sweet home!
    Erin Mavourneen! my own native home.

How sweet is the fragrance of your hills and your dales!
No reptiles disturb the sweet peace of your vales;
But the violet and primrose each brighten the scene,
And the shamrock still blooms in its own native green.
  Home, home; sweet, sweet home!
  Erin Mavourneen! my own native home.

Fond memory still clings to those youth-loving scenes,
Enchanting, yet saddening like Elysian dreams;
Erin Mavourneen! wherever I rove,
You're the home of my childhood, the land that I love.
  Home, home; sweet, sweet home!
  Erin Mavourneen! my own native home.

JUDITH McFADDEN'S REPLY TO PATRICK J. HACKERTY'S LETTER.*

My dear Misthur Cheeks, I have read your short letter—
 In troth, I am thinking it's quite long enough;
It's yourself I won't blame—you could do it no better,
 Or you ne'er would have penned such nonsensical stuff.

You call yourself Paddy—in troth, I disown you!
 You ne'er had a foot on the "Gem of the Sea;"
True Irish humor you never can touch at—
 You spalpeen! how dare you claim kindred with me?

When you talk of the girls, you belie my own Paddy—
 His heart it is honest; he still thinks of me;
He never will barter the love that he plighted—
 He loves his own Judy, his Cushlamachree!

* The above reply was written in answer to a scurrilous poem by a Cape May correspondent of the *Philadelphia Ledger*, in 1843.

Och! Misthur Cheeks, you have mighty fine larnin',—
A comfort, I'm sure, in the dullest of times;
And then for your poetry!—troth it is charming;—
You're quite a machine for the making of rhymes!

Your "forty pianny," your "board," and your "lumber,"
Such figures surpass e'en the genius of Moore; [guard,"
With your "Ah, Billy do," and "you impudent black-
What mighty fine times you have at the sea-shore.

You say that "some lines you must throw in the water:"
In troth, I am thinking that same they would need
Before that you write to your "jewel of Judies;"—
Your friends in this quarter your nonsense can't read.

My name it is Judy, I came from Killarney—
My own darlint Paddy he came from Tyrone;
When a letter he sends, it has none of the blarney—
My own darlint Paddy I'll never disown!

My dear Misthur Cheeks, I have finished my letter;
I'm sure you're not sorry to find it is done;
When you want to be witty, don't pass for a Paddy,
And you won't make a fool of your own mother's son.

ADDRESS OF THE CARRIERS OF THE CATHOLIC HERALD, JANUARY 1, 1851.

WE greet ye, patrons, on this festive day,
As Father Time pursues his onward way;
And, Fifty leaves us, with our hopes and fears,
To take its place in the long lapse of years—
Another link snapped from our little span.
We still rejoice, and welcome Fifty-One,
While all are swallowed in life's noiseless sea—
The great and small, the bondsman and the free;

And ere we touch on earth or earthly things,
We'll turn our thoughts unto the King of Kings.
Behold, oh man, the glorious works of God!
Each lovely flower that beautifies the sod,
With wild profusion decorates the plain
In simple grandeur o'er earth's wide domain;
Almighty Being! whose omnific hand
Created worlds and poised the sea and land,
Thy spirit moving o'er the cheerless night,
Arrayed in all the majesty of light;
Astonished angels hailed the first bright hour,
Sublimely grand by all-creative power—
From Thy bright throne the burning stars were hurled,
Globe upon globe, and world piled on world;
The mountain raised its stately brow to Thee,
And myriad tribes sprang forth in wanton glee.
What glorious wonders meet the curious eye!
Those mighty orbs that ornament the sky;
The sun and moon—the beauteous gods of light—
The king and queen of glorious day and night!
Behold the lightning shoot from cloud to cloud—
The crashing thunder rolling long and loud;
While angry oceans dash their billows high,
In fitful rage, to mock the lowering sky.
Behold the cataract, in its headlong sweep,
With awful grandeur hurrying to the deep—
A living picture of life's troubled sea,
Still rushing forward to eternity.
See Nature's gifts, luxuriantly profuse,
Start into life by heaven's mellow dews;
While gentle zephyrs sweetly sweep along
In sweet accordance with Creation's song.
The blushing rose, that sips the evening dew;
The pink and violet, with each varied hue;
The smiling lily, in the flowery dell;

The busy bee, that acts her part so well;
The crystal brook, that murmurs in the shade;—
Yes: all Creation, without human aid,
Reveals the truth, the hope of erring man,
To cheer his spirits through life's little span.
Thus sun and shade, the ocean and the air,
Confess, oh God, Thy presence everywhere;
Yet man, the master-piece of Thine own hand,
By folly blinded, searches sea and land
To gather dross that soon must fade away,
And with himself will molder and decay.
Oh Christian soul! to Bethlehem turn thine eyes,
Where man's Redeemer in a manger lies:
With faith and hope approach that poor abode
Where mercy veils the grandeur of a God,
And there adore, with gratitude and love,
Thy God, thy King, descended from above;
Nor throne of state, nor pageantry appears,
To crush thy hopes or awe the soul with fears;
But peace and love in heavenly accents flow
To ease the soul of every human woe.
Oh, happy day! thrice blessed be the morn
That watchful shepherds found their Saviour born,
And paid their homage at the early dawn,
When night had fled in darkness from the lawn;
And loud hosannahs echoed from the sky—
"Peace unto men! glory to God on high!"
And heavenly voices, sweetly borne along,
Sung sacred anthems of eternal song.
From polemics our trembling muse would shrink,
Could we forego the right we have to think,
And tamely gaze on error's fearful tide,
With noxious vapors spreading far and wide;
Beyond the pale of Mother Church we find
Discordant hosts, the sport of every wind,

Where falsehood seems to hold perpetual sway,
And leads her dupes in error's devious way.
When Luther first unchained the German mind,
And launched it forth, by folly doubly blind—
Proclaimed himself the chosen of the Lord
To teach and preach the Bible's sacred word,
And, Satan-like, forbidden fruits propose,
Bringing confusion with ten thousand woes,
That self-sent prophets, created by their art,
Might venture forth with reason for their chart;
And tens of thousands yield, the willing slaves
Of dreaming fools or dogmatizing knaves;
While every day brings forth some creed to view,
With Bible texts to prove their notions true!
Thus creeds and crimes are marching side by side,
And virtue mocked by arrogance and pride;
While cunning leads, with sanctimonious face,
Her willing dupes to some sequestered place,
To hear glad tidings from famed Timbuctoo—
Or, better still, a late converted Jew;
Retailing out some *tales* of Papal Rome,
Or shedding tears o'er backsliders at home.
Oh truth! thou art a two-edged sword indeed
To the poor wight that daily mends his creed;
And still must mend, in these progressive times,
And patch his faith as dunces patch their rhymes.
See England rent with agitation wild—
Religion scoffed, and liberty defiled,—
Where men stand forth, with more than bigot zeal,
To crush the truth 'neath despotism's heel:
How vain, oh man! thy puny efforts prove
When God's right hand protects His work of love!
E'en here "the saints" are roused to holy ire—
Each frowning camp has lit a signal fire,
And Sion's trumpet has proclaimed afar

The sacred duty of a gospel war;
They gird their loins with well-assorted tracts,
And smite the foe whenever he attacks,
Lest Papal Rome, or some tremendous name,
Should sweep away Columbia's fairest fame.
Poor human nature! how I would deplore
Thy sad mishaps on error's rugged shore,
Were there no star to lend its friendly light
To guide you safely through the murky night,
And lead you back within the sacred fold
Whose saving faith the prophets have foretold,
Where weary man in quiet may repose,
In heavenly peace, from every wind that blows.
Oh lovely temple! seated on a hill—
The glorious work of God's omnific skill;
In vain thy foes may rise in varied forms,
And jarring sects invoke tempestuous storms!
Let lightning flash, and angry thunders roll
In maddening fury, sweep from Pole to Pole:
Thou'lt rest secure while nations pass away;
A God has vowed thou shalt not go astray—
A Saviour left a Paraclete with thee,
To guide thee safely o'er life's troubled sea.
My muse shall next unveil the dark recess
Where crime appears in all its nakedness,
And hope stands shuddering at the breadth of crime
That seems to swell along the tide of time;
Intemperance we boldly mean to scan;—
Want in its train, a curse entailed on man—
From altars, raised for human sacrifice,
Blasphemous incense issues to the skies.
Her temples grand shut out the glorious light
With curtains red, like some unhallowed night:
There time's reversed—night turned into day;
There swearers swear, and cunning gamblers play;

'Tis there that poultry from our markets come,
And games are played for turkeys, geese and rum.
The assassin there receives his food for strife—
First takes his draught, then wields the deadly knife,
And hunts a brother whom he seeks to kill,
His conscience stifled by the accursed still.
'Tis there the father leaves his hard-earned toil,
And idle drones soon fatten on the spoil ;
The beggared mother, with a burning brain,
Her famished children call for bread in vain :
Their all is gone—their every hope has fled—
Their wants neglected : rum leaves naught for bread.
Intemperance !—thou wily fiend of hell !
The fairest prospects 'neath thy power fell :
The widowed mother and her hapless boy,
Her brightest hopes, her all thou didst destroy,
And cast them forth upon a barren waste—
Their *bosom's love* by every crime disgraced—
A prey to want in all its varied forms,
A fragile bark tossed by resistless storms ;
Like birds of flight, for ever forced to roam—
Repulsed by friends, cast from a beggared home.
Behold yon maniac in his dreary cell,
His reason wrecked by some unhallowed spell—
With steady hand he caught the accursed bowl
That quenched the light of reason from his soul ;
The haggard face—the agitated frame—
The tattered drunkard, dead to sense and shame,
Stalks forth to mock the dignity of man :
A useless blank fills up his little span.
The brute that roams abroad fills well his place,
Commits no crime that can his kind disgrace ;
Not so the drunkard in his wild disputes—
Our muse must class him 'neath the lowest brutes !

NATIONAL TEMPERANCE SONG.*

DEDICATED TO FRANCIS COOPER, ESQ.

HAIL! birthday of freedom!—when, in glory arrayed,
The Star-spangled Banner its beauties displayed
    O'er the land of the free and the home of the brave;
The fair Sun of Freedom beamed bright in the West,
The Temperance Gem sparkling high on his crest,
Shedding a halo round Liberty's shores,
Where the Eagle, unfettered, triumphantly soars
    O'er the land of the free and the home of the brave!

The Temple of Liberty ever shall stand
While Union and Temperance go hand in hand,
    O'er the land of the free and the home of the brave:
The bright boon of freedom to us has been given
Like an angel of mercy descending from heaven,
Dispelling the darkness of tyranny's night,
And disclosing the Eagle encircled in light,
    O'er the land of the free and the home of the brave!

Then flourish for ever our temperance cause—
Best bulwark of freedom! best guardian of laws!
    In the land of the free and the home of the brave.
Hail! Temple of Freedom!—Hail! Temple of Fame!
Inscribed on thy crest is our WASHINGTON's name;
Hibernia has given a Montgomery to thee,
Who sealed with his blood the great cause of the free,
    In this land of the free and bright home of the brave.

SONG OF THE EXILE.†

HAIL! thrice happy day!—to the exile endearing,
    As he wanders afar o'er life's troubled sea;

* Music composed and sung by B. Cross, Esq., in the grand saloon of the Museum, at the Catholic Temperance Celebration on the 5th of July, 1842.
† Composed for the celebration of St. Patrick's Day by the Penna. Catholic Total Abstinence Society, held in the Philadelphia Museum, March 17, 1843.

And sacred's the tie that still binds him to Erin,
　　While the pulse of his heart throbs for Cushlamachree.

No hills are so green as my own native mountains;
　　No valleys so fertile, no flowers so fair;
No nectar more pure than the crystal-like fountains,
　　Whose murmurs are fanned by thine own balmy air.

Behold our loved Erin, in bold agitation,
　　Combating with despots to sever her chains—
Proclaiming aloud that she must be a nation,
　　Free as the breezes that sweep o'er her plains!

Nations have sunk 'neath the lash of oppression—
　　Their glory departed, all shrouded in gloom;
Whilst Erin Mavourneen, resisting aggression,
　　Thy spirit ne'er slumbered in slavery's tomb.

Oh! harp of my country!—the pride of her sages—
　　In vain would the tyrant thy numbers control:
Thou'rt the gift of our fathers—the boast of past ages,—
　　Thy music still lives in each Irishman's soul.

Then hail to thee, Erin! wherever I wander
　　My spirit still lingers around thy loved shore,
Where Nature appears in her own native grandeur,
　　And thy sons are as brave as their fathers of yore.

———

OH! BLEST BE THE LAND OF MY FATHERS.

Air—"Lamentation of Aughrim."

Oh! blest be the land of my fathers;
　　Thy spirit for ever be free,—
Blest be thy name, oh Hibernia!
　　Thou beautiful gem of the sea.

I'll take down my harp from the willow,
    Though broken each chord of its frame:
Its notes shall be heard o'er the billow,
    Resounding, loved Erin, thy fame.

Thy spirit shall waken its numbers,
    Though banished beyond the dark wave;
Proclaiming the deeds of thy chieftains,
    Who're sleeping the sleep of the brave!

Thy tyrant may boast of his glory,
    And bigotry slander thy name—
Thy virtues, loved Erin, in story,
    Will cover the Saxon with shame.

ON THE GREAT REPEAL MEETING HELD ON TARA HILL, AUGUST 15, 1843.

Oh Erin, my country! resplendent in story;
    Redeemed, disenthralled, after ages of woe;
We hail the first dawn of thy long-faded glory
    As in grandeur it beams o'er thy insolent foe.
The cry of oppression—the widow's lone wailing,
    Ascended on high from thy long-injured land;
And, now, the grim tyrant in terror stands quailing,
    For God in his vengeance has palsied his hand.

Then gather, ye millions, on the green hills of Tara,
    Where the chieftains of old in their glory have stood,
And sever the chains of the modern Pharaoh,
    Whose chalice is filled with the nation's best blood;
Strike but a blow, and your chains they are riven—
    " Remember the glories of Brian the brave;"
Freedom's your right—'tis the gift of high heaven:
    From your Emerald Gem blot the brand of the slave!

The day-star of Freedom bursts o'er thy horizon—
  The Eagle of Liberty peacefully scars ;
While millions of freemen indignant are rising,
  Free as the surges that sweep round thy shores.
Behold thy O'Connell : he lays the foundation
  Of honor and freedom, loved Erin, for thee ;
We'll behold thee, once more, take thy rank as a nation,
  And thy harp wake to freedom for Cushlamachree.

Hail ! Queen of the Ocean !—thou hast for a dower
  A jewel preserved through oppression's dark night ;
The lone winds that sigh through thy long-ruined towers
  Waft back thy glories like visions of light.
May the God of our fathers protect thee from danger,
  And grant every blessing, Mavourneen, to thee,
Is the prayer of the exile in the land of the stranger
  As his spirit is wafted to Cushlamachree.

ON THE ARREST OF DANIEL O'CONNELL.

  YE exiled Irishmen, arise !
    Behold the Emerald of the Sea
  Arrayed to win the golden prize—
    Her native jewel, Liberty !
  Mavourneen Erin's onward now :
    Her sons are temperate and brave ;
  No crime pollutes her spotless brow—
    God ne'er designed her for a slave.

  The spirit of her mighty dead
    Has burst the fetters of the tomb ;
  Her blood-stained tyrant stands in dread,
    While gazing on impending doom !

Behold that martyred patriot host
   Whose cry ascends to outraged heaven,
And echoes round her sea-bound coast,
   That Erin's chains shall now be riven.

Up! Irishmen: up, one and all!
   Curse on the heartless renegade
Who cannot hear his country's call,
   Or would his country's cause degrade!
Oh! may the glorious sun ne'er shine
   Above the traitor's guilty head!
May hell's dark spectres all combine
   To hover round his midnight bed!

Up! Irishmen, where'er you roam
   In exile, far o'er earth's domain;
Arise! for freedom, friends, and home—
   Strike off the despot's galling chain!
Swear, by the memory of the past,
   And by your Emmett's lonely tomb,
Or by the shades of Mullaghmast,
   That you shall seal the tyrant's doom!

Swear by the glories of your Brian,
   And by the deeds his valor won—
By the deep wail of widow Ryan,
   While weeping o'er her murdered son!
Swear by the burning tears that start
   From the lone exile's wistful eyes,
While every feeling of his heart
   Is uttered forth in bitter sighs;

Invoke that God who still can save—
   Send up a prayer to Mercy's throne,
Who ne'er has willed to be a slave
   An image fashioned to his own.

Oh God! what crimes—what awful deeds!
  What scenes of blood—what floods of tears!
My country clothed in mourning weeds
  For seven hundred harrowing years!

Mavourneen Erin! thou hast stood
  Like Israel in Egyptian chains,
While tyrant hate hath lapped thy blood—
  In triumph mocked thy plaintive strains:
Yet thou hast hoped in Israel's God,
  Who smote in twain the troubled sea;
And now, behold the mystic rod
  O'Connell wields for Liberty!

Oh! Emerald gem, we still revere
  Thy ancient fame, thy classic lore;
Home of our youth! to memory dear—
  We pine in exile from thy shore.
We pledge our liberty and life
  To stand by thee—come weal, come woe;
And side by side in battle strife
  To crush thy unrelenting foe!

ADIEU TO LOUGH SWILLY.

Air—"Banks of the Dee."

Adieu to Lough Swilly! from thee I must wander,—
  Sweet scene of contentment! how dear to my soul!—
Where Nature appears in her own native grandeur,
  And thy blue, briny waters transparently roll.
On thy moss-covered banks the blue-bells are growing;
The violet and primrose, twin-sisters, are blowing;
And the sea-shells are kissed by the bright waters flowing
  Round the scene of my childhood—oh Cushlamachree!

Nature exhausted her riches, her powers,
  To make thee, loved Erin, the gem of the sea ;
She strewed thy green mounts with the fairest of flowers,
  The shamrock left blooming forever with thee !
She viewed thy young beauties with heart-felt emotion—
Foretold thou shouldst e'er be the patriot's devotion ;
And crowned thee, forever, bright queen of the ocean,—
  Oh ! time-honored title of Cushlamachree !

Fond memory oft flies on the wings of affection
  To the scenes of our childhood, first home of our youth,
Where, nursed by the care of a mother's protection,
  We lisped the first accents of virtue and truth.
Fond memory oft flies in the fulness of feeling—
Our thoughts, like a wizard, enchantingly stealing
To mingle with those where oft we have been kneeling,
  Around thy pure altars, oh Cushlamachree !

YE SONS OF HIBERNIA.

Air—" Sons of Fingal."

Ye sons of Hibernia ! awake from your slumbers,
  And sever the chains that have bound you so long ;
Depend upon God and the strength of your numbers—
  Let the war-cry of Freedom enliven your song !

Your fields they are fertile—your valleys are blooming—
  Your daughters are fair, and your sons they are brave ;
While tyrants, for ages your heart's blood consuming,
  Have branded your name with the stamp of a slave.

Remember the deeds of your fathers in story—
  Remember the chieftains of Tara's famed hall !
Cast but a glimpse on your long-faded glory,
  And burst the sad chains that your children enthrall.

Let the voice of your chieftains re-echo like thunder;
Let the standard of green be unfurled once more!—
Your oppressors affrighted, beholding with wonder,
Will vanish in terror from Erin's loved shore.

In vain will all despots contend with your power—
In vain will Britannia rivet your chains:
Freedom, loved Erin, your own native flower,
For ages has bloomed on your mountains and plains.

The hearts of your exiles still beat with emotion—
Loved Erin! their spirits oft hover round thee;
To them thou'rt a queen—Oh! bright gem of the ocean,
They sigh for thy freedom, sweet Cushlamachree.

OH! LAND OF MY SIRES.*

AIR—"Paddy Whack."

OH! land of my sires—I gaze with delight
As thy Sun-burst † of ages breaks forth from the gloom,
That oppression had wrapt in the shadows of night,
And consigned to oblivion in slavery's tomb.
We behold thee arise in the might of a nation,
Though the tyrant for ages thy Shamrock hath trod;
Yet unsullied and pure as the day of Creation,
When an Emerald thou camest from the finger of God.

Then flourish for ever, my own native Erin!
Thy daughters are fair and thy sons true and brave;
Liberty's friend, and no tyranny fearing,
Thy soil never fostered a coward or slave.

* Composed for and dedicated to the Pennsylvania Catholic Total Abstinence Society, and sung at their celebration on the 17th of March, 1844.

† A name given by the ancient Irish to the National Standard.

Hail! Chief of our Isle! though in exile we wander,
    Our prayer of affection is offered for thee;
Let tyranny rage and dark bigotry slander—
    Thou'rt the Day-star of hope to our Cushlamachree.
When Boreas bursts forth on the breast of old ocean,
    The frail bark may quiver before the dread gale:
Not so our O'Connell; in the midst of commotion,
    He's the Pilot of Freedom to loved Innisfail!

    Then flourish for ever, my own native Erin!
        Thy daughters are fair and thy sons true and brave;
    Liberty's friend, and no tyranny fearing,
        Thy soil never fostered a coward or slave.

Thy harp, long neglected, awakes from its slumbers,
    The sad song of sorrows departed from thee;
While the war-cry of Freedom enlivens its numbers
    With the soul-stirring anthem of Cushlamachree.
Then, Irishmen, up! in the land of the stranger,
    While tyrants and traitors your country assail:
Stand by old Erin in her moments of danger—
    Behold in her van the "Red Hand" of O'Neil!

    Then flourish for ever, my own native Erin!
        Thy daughters are fair and thy sons true and brave;
    Liberty's friend, and no tyranny fearing,
        Thy soil never fostered a coward or slave.

TO ERIN.

On! Erin, my country! once more thou shalt flourish,
    And thy sons be as free as the surge round thy shore;
The fair gem of Freedom long, long didst thou cherish,
    With a feeling as deep as the heart's inmost core.

Firm as thyself in the midst of old ocean,
  And pure as the run of thy murmuring rills,
Are the hearts of thy exiles, with filial devotion,
  As in spirit they roam o'er thy daisy-clad hills.

The Star-spangled Banner is fitfully streaming,
  To cheer thee, Mavourneen, 'midst tyranny's gloom!
And the day-star of Freedom in splendor is beaming,
  To light thee, loved Erin, from slavery's tomb.

No longer the Lion of merciless Britain
  Shall prowl undisturbed o'er thy mountains and plains;
And the long wished-for epitaph soon shall be written,
  As thy harp wakes to Freedom in soul-stirring strains.

———

ANSWER TO THE SHAN VAN VOCHT OF '46.

Oh! my brother, bide your time,
          Says the Shan Van Vocht;
Oh! my brother, bide your time,
          Says the Shan Van Vocht;
Oh! my brother, bide your time,
For patience is sublime,
While rashness is a crime,
          Says the Shan Van Vocht.

Oh! my brother, wait a while,
          Says the Shan Van Vocht;
Oh! my brother, wait a while,
          Says the Shan Van Vocht;
Oh! my brother, wait a while—
Heaven yet will kindly smile
Upon our own green isle,
          Says the Shan Van Vocht.

There's hope for you and me,
       Says the Shan Van Vocht;
There's hope for you and me,
       Says the Shan Van Vocht;
There's hope for you and me;
For old Erin shall be free
As the waves on yon blue sea,
       Says the Shan Van Vocht.

My heart's not troubled now,
       Says the Shan Van Vocht;
My heart's not troubled now,
       Says the Shan Van Vocht;
My heart's not troubled now,
For my sons have made a vow
To wipe slavery from my brow,
       Says the Shan Van Vocht.

I have sons now growing old,
       Says the Shan Van Vocht;
I have sons now growing old,
       Says the Shan Van Vocht;
I have sons now growing old,
Virtuous, wise, and bold—
Unbought by Saxon gold,
       Says the Shan Van Vocht.

I have sons that want to fight,
       Says the Shan Van Vocht;
I have sons that want to fight,
       Says the Shan Van Vocht;
I have sons that want to fight—
In troth, I know they're right!
Och! they're my ould heart's delight,
       Says the Shan Van Vocht.

I have a word to say,
> Says the Shan Van Vocht,
To my children far away,
> Says the Shan Van Vocht;
Remember your old mother!
Oh! be kind to one another,
And angry feelings smother,
> Says the Shan Van Vocht.

Oh! look beyond the wave,
> Says the Shan Van Vocht;
See the struggling of the brave!
> Says the Shan Van Vocht;
Stand by old ocean's Queen,
While your native hills are green
Or a shamrock can be seen,
> Says the Shan Van Vocht.

LINES ON THE PROCESSION OF THE PENNSYL-VANIA CATHOLIC TOTAL ABSTINENCE SOCIETY, ON 4TH JULY, 1842.

YES: onward! myriad thousands,
On our glorious festive day!
With hearts of lasting gratitude
Your annual tribute pay;
With banners proudly waving
And the spirit-stirring drum,
And true hearts, vowed to free the land
From soul-destroying rum.

Yes! let the silver clarion sound,
And banners proudly wave,
If you can save a brother from
A drunkard's hideous grave;

Yes: onward! myriad thousands --
  Send the hallowed pledge around,
Until the viper finds no place
  On consecrated ground!

You have the blessing of your God
  To aid your glorious cause;
While Virtue feels herself secure
  With liberty and laws.
Then hail! thrice hail! our natal day,
  When old and young rejoice,
Where tyrant kings and titled lords
  Raise not their regal voice;

But man, in all the plentitude
  Conferred by Deity,
Enjoyeth all that Earth can give—
  The jewel, Liberty!
The Eagle towers in his strength,
  Unscathed by foreign wars;
While peace and plenty smile around,
  Beneath our Stripes and Stars.

RUINS OF ST. AUGUSTINE'S CHURCH.

Destroyed by a mob, called Native Americans, May 10, 1844.

Oh! say, have you heard through the stillness of night,
  The "Natives'" loud yell, shouting o'er their dark doings;
While the flames from yon church are affording them light
  For rapine and plunder, while its altar's in ruins?
            Yes! the church's red glare
            Showed the fiends that were there,
            Uniting to fire our houses of prayer!
Then who dare deny that those "Natives" were braves,
Whose courage uprooted the dead from their graves?

Have you heard the dread shout that in triumph arose,
  When from the high dome fell the sign of salvation?
Thus the Saviour was hailed in the midst of his foes,
  When the Jews sought his life "for the good of the
      How vain was that yell   [nation."
      O'er the Cross as it fell—
'Twas but the wild tumult that echoes through hell!
Then who dare deny that those "Natives" were braves,
Whose courage uprooted the dead from their graves?

Oh City of Penn!—oh shame! where's thy blush?
  See the Temple of God stand in sad desolation—
See bigots uniting their efforts to crush
  The church of those heroes* who fought for this nation!
      How inglorious his fame
      Who boasts without shame
Of a cause that has shrouded God's temples in flame!
Behold! "THE LORD SEETH" the deeds of that night,†
And the God of our fathers will judge his cause right.

LINES ON THE NATIVITY.

HAIL! lowly manger;—hail! humble abode,
That sheltered a Virgin, a Saviour, a God!
What hand shall transcribe on the pages of story,
  As heaven unfolded its portals of light—
Revealing to shepherds bright legions of glory,
  Chanting hosannas in the stillness of night.

Christians, rejoice! your Redeemer is born;
Salvation's revealed on this thrice happy morn!

* Barry, Lafayette, Carroll, and a host of others.
† "THE LORD SEETH."—These words were in gilt letters over the altar.
Notwithstanding the destruction of everything, the gilt letters remained
unharmed by water or fire, which was considered marvellous at the time.

For God, in his mercy, to man has descended,
  Revealing his glory to nations afar;
Who, with faith and obedience most happily blended,
  Hasten to Jesus 'neath Bethlehem's star.

Hail! Virgin of Virgins!—by an angel addressed
With, "hail! full of grace"—above all women blessed;
Hail! Virgin, whom nations, with filial devotion,
  Still call their Mother;—oh! list to our prayer:
Obtain for us mercy on life's troubled ocean—
  Oh! take us, sweet Mother, to thy holy care.

LAMENT.

COLD is the grave where my dear wife lies sleeping—
  No longer a guardian she stands by my side!
Lonely, ah! lonely, sad vigils I'm keeping,
  For Death claimed his own, and has made her his bride.
        How vain is my mourning!
        There's no hope returning—
  For Death claimed his own, and has made her his bride.

Like the mist of the morning, she vanished for ever;
  Her soul winged its way to the God of all love;—
An angel of mercy, beyond the dark river,
  Pointed her pathway to mansions above.
        How vain is my mourning!
        There's no hope returning—
  For Death claimed his own, and has made her his bride.

www.ingramcontent.com/pod-product-compliance
Lightning Source LLC
Chambersburg PA
CBHW031320280626
47169CB00019B/2520